DATE DUE

JE 10 '92			
NO 30 '94			
MY 2 6 '95			
OC 19 '09			

COME OUT
INTO THE SUN

COME OUT
INTO THE SUN
Poems New and Selected

ROBERT FRANCIS

THE UNIVERSITY OF MASSACHUSETTS PRESS

WORKS OF ROBERT FRANCIS

Stand With Me Here
Valhalla and Other Poems
The Sound I Listened For
We Fly Away
The Face Against the Glass
The Orb Weaver
Come Out Into the Sun
The Satirical Rogue on Poetry

Library of Congress Catalog Card Number 65-26243

Manufactured in the United States of America

Second Printing, 1968

For Joseph Langland
prime mover and
first friend of this book

Some of the NEW POEMS originally appeared in magazines. Grateful acknowledgment is made to the editors of the following: *Commonweal* (1965); *Harvard Alumni Bulletin* (1960); *Kentucky Writing, Number 3* (1960); *Lyric* (1953, 1961); *The Massachusetts Review* (1961, 1962, 1965); *The New York Times* (1965); *Syracuse 10* (1961); *Transatlantic Review* (1959); *The Virginia Quarterly Review* (1965). "Come Out Into the Sun" appeared originally in *The New Yorker*. "Delicate the Toad" was first published in the Summer 1964 issue of *The New-England Galaxy*.

A selection of twenty-nine poems in POEMS 1950–1960 is included from *The Orb Weaver*, by Robert Francis, by permission of the Wesleyan University Press. "The Orb Weaver" and "Desiring to Give All" appeared originally in *Forum*.

EARLIER POEMS is comprised of selections from *Stand With Me Here, Valhalla and Other Poems*, and *The Sound I Listened For*.

• Contents •

EARLIER POEMS

NEW
POEMS

Sniper

The tree becomes him, he becomes the tree—
A visionary whom the world can't see.

His solitude makes sense.
His leisure is immense.

Least organized of men and most unknown,
His deaths are singular, including his own.

How lean, how lyrical
A life. A fame how small.

Old Men

Weigh too much or weigh
Too little,

Settle into woodchucks or take
A fancy

To be feather-weight birds.
Very seldom

However you catch one singing.
As merchandise

Old men go very cheap
Marked down

Marked down year after year
After year.

Watching Gymnasts
For P.T.

Competing not so much with one another
As with perfection
    They follow follow as voices in a fugue
    A severe music.

Something difficult they are making clear
Like the crack teacher
    Demonstrating their paradigms until
    The dumb see.

How flower-light they toss themselves, how light
They toss and fall
    And flower-light, precise, and arabesque
    Let their praise be.

Stellaria

Your five white, frost-white
Petals and plum-purple stamens
Stellaria, for a sharp eye
For a fond eye— who
But the botanist ever sees?

Your foliage is weed familiar
But your flower is almost
Like a fairy princess invisible.
Better so. Those who escape
Man's notice escape man's scorn.

To the most proper garden
You come uninvited and unthanked
Before or after the planted
Plants, schooled for an early
Winter and a late spring.

Easier larger flowers than you
I would not slander. Under
The sun all are equal.
And yet your very smallness
Like modesty is a jewel.

For I am not unprejudiced.
The unpromoted flower I prefer
Far from a florist window
As you, starwort, are far.
How cool, unqualified, your gaze.

Coin Diver (Funchal)

He takes it first with his eye like a sparrow hawk
all the way down to water and a little way under.

Tossed out of heaven a dime is less than a dime
but silver larger than life in the diver's palm.

He holds it up. Larger than life and cleaner
than any money has a right to look.

He taps his forehead to salute the donor
who over the rail from under the clouds peers.

Another coin cuts water. Cat-wise he waits,
he waits for stillness and a certain depth

Then with the least fuss possible he follows
but loses it this time, poor deep blue devil.

But does he? Does he? His innocent palms are empty.
He grins: the silver safe between his toes.

Dolphin

In mythology the restraint shown by dolphins
Is praiseworthy. Foregoing the preposterous they are
Content with only a little more than
Truth. They do what actual-factual dolphins
Have been known to do in times
Past or times present: pilot a ship
Or ride a small boy bareback smiling.

Conversely real dolphins seem influenced by myth
As if the overheard story of Arion
Could furnish endless inspiration in a dolphin's
Daily life. Such was Opo of Opononi,
Opo of the Antipodes, Opo who let
Non-dolphin fellow-bathers stroke his back.
And when he died New Zealand mourned.

Having achieved, after how many ages, dry
Land, these beasts returned to live successfully
With sharks and devilfish. Having achieved dry
Land they achieved the sea. And this
Was long long before the first myth.
Today the uninhabitable for us, thank Dolphin,
Is that much less uninhabitable and inhospitable.

In weather foggy-shaggy in mid-Atlantic
Watching their water sports, tumbling, leap-frog
Who could be wholly in the doldrums
Doleful? A rough sea chuckles with dolphins
And a smooth sea dimples. Delft blue.
Delphinium-blue blooming with white morning-glories.
The sea relaxes. They tickle the sea.

Love Conquered by a Dolphin could equally
Be called A Dolphin Conquered by Love.
The seabeast holds the god coiled

But his moony upward-rolling eyes tell
Who is the more hopelessly caught. Preposterous?
The antique sculptor shrugs: with so ravishing
A god what could poor dolphin do?

From the large brain intricate as man's
And slightly larger one could predict intelligence
And from intelligence superior to a dog's,
An ape's, an elephant's, one could predict
Language, but where is science to predict
(Much less explain) benevolence such as Opo's,
Opo riding a small boy bareback smiling?

Nothing less than forgiveness dolphins teach us
If we, miraculously, let ourselves be taught.
Enduring scientific torture no dolphin has yet
(With experimental electrodes hammered into its skull)
In righteous wrath turned on its tormentors.
What will science ever find more precious?
The sea relaxes. They bless the sea.

Ireland

which the sea refuses
to recognize as bona fide
land, the sea and all her watery clouds

and all her mewing gulls
"white craws as white as snaw"
that sweep, that sweep, that sweep

warm winter into cool summer
"rather cloudy, but with bright
periods in many places this morning"—

Ireland whose weather imitates
bird flightiness, imitates life,
imitates above all the Irish.

Time and the Sergeant

To take us in, bully and bawl us
Out was his official
Pleasure.

And he was beautifully built for it,
That buffed brass hair, that
Tuba voice

And those magnificent legs on which
He rocked he rocked. He never
Bent a knee.

How is the anal-oriented humor now?
Fresh and exuberant
As ever?

Or has Old Bastard Time touched
Even you, Sergeant,
Even you?

Hogwash

The tongue that mothered such a metaphor
Only the purest purist could despair of.

Nobody ever called swill sweet but isn't
Hogwash a daisy in a field of daisies?

What beside sports and flowers could you find
To praise better than the American language?

Bruised by American foreign policy
What shall I soothe me, what defend me with

But a handful of clean unmistakable words—
Daisies, daisies, in a field of daisies?

Eagle Plain

The American eagle is not aware he is
the American eagle. He is never tempted
to look modest.

When orators advertise the American eagle's
virtues, the American eagle is not listening.
This is his virtue.

He is somewhere else, he is mountains away
but even if he were near he would never
make an audience.

The American eagle never says he will serve
if drafted, will dutifully serve etc. He is
not at our service.

If we have honored him we have honored one
who unequivocally honors himself by
overlooking us.

He does not know the meaning of magnificent.
Perhaps we do not altogether either
who cannot touch him.

Icicles

Only a fierce
Coupling begets them
Fire and freezing

Only from violent
Yet gentle parents
Their baroque beauty

Under the sun
Their life passes
But wait awhile

Under the moon
They are finished
Works of art

Poems in print
Yet pity them
Only by wasting

Away they grow
And their death
Is pure violence.

The Articles of War

Do I forget the Articles of War?
Herded into a bare mess hall
We stood against the unaccommodating wall
Or squatted on the floor
To hear what they could hang or shoot us for.

All of us green, but one greener by half,
Green enough to stand out in the crowd,
Asked (since questions were allowed)
"Can you resign from the Army?" The laugh
We gave him! How we hooted at the calf!

Hootable, I suppose, was Henry Thoreau
Whose equally unaccommodating fate
It was to try to disentangle from the State.
But Liberty would not let him go.
The State said: "Henry, no."

Somebody next, who knows? may try
Resigning from the human race,
Somebody aghast at history,
Haunted by hawk's eyes in the human face.
Somebody—could it be I?

The Packing Case

When Van Loon packed the human race
Neatly inside a packing case,
Dimensions one-half cubic mile—

When Van Loon poised the packing case
Over the upper edge of space
And teased and teetered it a while—

No one outside, no one bereft,
Not even one old Noah left
To mosey to the Land of Nod—

Sing lullaby—when history dived
And only geography survived—
Who mercifully breathed Thank God?

Reading Gravestones

I

These granite authorities on death
contradict one another as only
authorities can.

II

Squirrels in the oaks seem never
to have heard of death—
authorities on acorns.

III

After the mourners leave, the flowers
they leave could teach them
how to weep.

IV

Strange how the stones as they
grow heavier and more Egyptian
grow more taciturn.

V

Snow buries them a second time
as if one Christian burial
were not enough.

Delicate the Toad

Delicate the toad
Sits and sips
The evening air.

He is satisfied
With dust, with
Color of dust.

A hopping shadow
Now, and now
A shadow still.

Laugh, you birds
At one so
Far from flying

But have you
Caught, among small
Stars, his flute?

Idyl of Lake Reedy

Others have moved the heavens
To move but what other
With more idyllic ease (herself
Unmoving) than Miss Lillie Stoate
Who merely sat by water?

Any considerable body of water
Would serve if Miss Lillie
Happily were sitting beside it.
Simply sitting there. What was
It Brancusi said about simplicity?

Miss Lillie Stoate from Mississippi
Came to fruit-growing Florida
And sat beside Lake Reedy
Several hours several successive days.
Noted, she brought her umbrella.

A big black one undoubtedly.
In this foreseeable unforeseeable world
Any woman of sixty-seven
Knows she needs ample protection.
She also brought her knitting

Most probably though not noted.
Difficult indeed to picture her
Without it—sitting and knitting
Knitting and sitting. Oh, sometimes
She simply sat and watched

The stilt-legged water-birds
Dip and dive and dimple
A surface otherwise all unruffled
And uneventful. Was Lake Reedy
Named for somebody named Reedy?

However so, at this distance
We are privileged to picture
Lake Reedy a really reedy
Lake fringed with water-weeds
And bulrushes and various grasses.

Prayer must have proved unavailing,
Prayer as if to waken
The Deity from afternoon napping.
Miss Lillie did not need,
Did not presume, to pray.

And what of cloud-compelling
Science? Had *that* been tried?
If so, we can legitimately
Label Miss Lillie Stoate both
Pre-scientific and post-scientific.

When the very first raindrops
A little hesitantly perhaps began
To fall on Lake Reedy
And on Miss Lillie, began
To stipple the bland surface

And the slightest possible stir
Of air to ripple it
She put down her knitting
And put up her umbrella
But kept on sitting. Why

Should she depart? Why should
She hurry away? The patter
Of drops on her umbrella
Was pleasant to listen to
Becoming more and more musical.

Only when it was clear
Beyond cavil that the rain
Meant business did Miss Lillie
Rise sighing, ah, surely less
From exertion than from fulfillment.

Aphrodite as History

Though the marble is ancient
It is only an ancient
Copy and though the lost
Original was still more ancient
Still it was not Praxiteles
Only a follower of Praxiteles
And Praxiteles was not first.

Emergence

If you have watched a moulting mantis
With exquisite precision and no less
Exquisite patience, extricate itself
Leaf-green and like a green leaf clinging
Little by little, leg by leg
Out of its chitin shell, you likewise know
How one day coaxes itself out of another
Slowly, slowly by imperceptible degrees
Of gray, and having fully emerged, pauses
To dry its wings.

Thoreau in Italy

Lingo of birds was easier than the lingo of peasants—
they were elusive, though, the birds, for excellent reasons.
He thought of Virgil, Virgil who wasn't there to chat with.

History he never forgave for letting Latin
lapse into Italian, a renegade jabbering
musical enough but not enough to call music.

So he conversed with stones, imperial and papal.
Even the preposterous popes he could condone
a moment for the clean arrogance of their inscriptions.

He asked the Italians only to leave him in the past
alone, but this was what they emphatically never did.
Being the present, they never ceased to celebrate it.

Something was always brushing him on the street, satyr
or saint—impossible to say which the more foreign.
At home he was called touchy; here he knew he was.

Impossible to say. The dazzling nude with sex
lovingly displayed like carven fruit, the black
robe sweeping a holy and unholy dust.

Always the flesh whether to lacerate or kiss—
conspiracy of fauns and clerics smiling back
and forth at each other acquiescently through leaves.

Caught between wan monastic mountains wearing the tonsure
and the all-siren, ever-dimpling sea, he saw
(how could he fail?) at heart geography to blame.

So home to Concord where (as he might have known he would)
he found the Italy he wanted to remember.
Why had he sailed if not for the savour of returning?

An Italy distilled of all extreme, conflict,
collusion—an Italy without the Italians—
in whose green context he could con again his Virgil.

In cedar he read cypress, in the wild apple, olive.
His hills would stand up favorably to the hills of Rome.
His arrowheads could hold their own with art Etruscan.

And Walden clearly was his Mediterranean
whose infinite colors were his picture gallery.
How far his little boat transported him—how far.

Comedian Body

Forgive comedian body
For featuring the bawdy.

For instance the poor fanny
So basic and so funny.

Forgive the penis pun
That perfect two-in-one.

Forgive the blowing nose.
Forgive the ten clown toes

And all the Noah's zoo
Of two by two by two.

Forgive a joke wherein
All love and art begin.

Forgive the incarnate word
Divine, obscene, absurd.

Old Man's Confession of Faith

The blowing wind I let it blow,
I let it come, I let it go.

Always it has my full permission.
Such is my doctrinal position.

I let it blow, I more than let it,
I comfort give, aid and abet it.

Young long ago I would resist it.
Today, full circle, I assist it.

When the wind blows, I let it blow me.
Where the wind goes, why there I go me.

I teach the wind no indoor manners
But egg it on with flags and banners.

Whether it expedite or slow me
When the wind blows I let it blow me.

Blow long, blow late, blow wild, blow crazy
Blow paper bag, blow dust, blow daisy

Blow east, blow west—I let it blow.
I never never tell it No.

The Black Hood

You don't remember—or perhaps you do—
The man who hid his head in the black hood
And worked a miracle or thought he could
To prove them one: the beautiful and the true?
He made you look, for once, the way you should:
Highly presentable yet no less you.

How we elude the harsh antinomies.
In love with two worlds that can scarcely meet
How human to claim both, the best of both,
To ask for dream fulfillment *and* for truth,
A likeness, but a flattering likeness, please.
Oh, never call the heart's desire deceit.

We could be less, a shade the less, to blame
Because our betters nobly do the same:
Bland Plato pulling on his long black hood
To find identical the true, the good,
Proving the world is better than we know
Because we and great Plato wish it so.

How much hood-hiding not to say hood-winking,
Yet with what lofty motives we deceive.
How many times we think that we are thinking
In making believe we do not make believe.
We spend to save—or do we save to spend?
We are the Russians' enemy and friend.

If I were gold, I would endow a chair
On principle if not for practical good
For someone who could tell us how to tell
Clean truth from trick, someone who dared to tell,
Someone as uncommitted as fresh air,
Without a trace, without a thread, of hood.

Good God, what have I said? And who am I?
You might suppose me totally unacquainted
With the dark mysteries of Paradox.
I am a poet, minor. Or I try.
If all duplicity deserves a pox,
Then I myself am tainted, more than tainted.

I marry freedom to fastidious form.
I trust the spirit in the arms of sense.
I can contrive a calm from any storm.
My art, my business is ambivalence.
In every poem by me on my shelf
Confidentially yours I hide myself.

Thus do I praise duplicity and damn it.
I hate equivocation and I am it.
True though I hanker for simplicity,
The concept of plain truth, plain simple truth,
Seems quaint and dubious as a wisdom tooth.
How guileless that black hood compared to me.

Written for and read at the literary exercises of the Harvard Chapter of Phi Beta Kappa, June 13, 1960.

The Forced Forsythia

Even the florist if he dreams of force
(Dreaming of sudden fortune) is only dreaming.
His warmth, his moisture, must be love, of course.

Women, true, have been goaded by the gods
In guise of bull or swan. Still they lack power,
The very gods, to force a flower to flower.

A yellow any more yellow would dazzle eyes.
Loaded, bursting with it, the wands are bowing
While snow peers through the glass in cold surprise.

Edith Sitwell Assumes the Role of Luna
or
If You Know What I Mean Said the Moon

Who (said the Moon)
Do you think I am and precisely who
Pipsqueak, are you

With your uncivil liberties
To do as you damn please?
Boo!

I am the serene
Moon (said the Moon).
Don't touch me again.

To your poking telescopes,
Your peeking eyes
I have long been wise.

Science? another word
For monkeyshine.
You heard me.

Get down, little man, go home,
Back where you come from,
Bah!

Or my gold will be turning green
On me (said the Moon)
If you know what I mean.

Eagle Caged

Uneagled in his coop
Listless, lackluster
His idle feathers droop
Like a feather duster.

Wing that assumed the sky
Forgets to stir.
Even the diamond eye
Is prisoner.

The wan inner sheath
Closes, uncloses.
He blinks vaguely at death
And dying, dozes.

Cinna

FOURTH CITIZEN: *Tear him for his bad verses.*

You were mistaken, Cinna, from the start.
First, to be single among sound married men,
Second, to make light of it. You were wrong there
And wrong again
On that red evening to have risked a breath of air.

But what was most conspicuously bad,
Being a poet, to let the thing be known.
And to have a name another man could have and had.
That, and to walk alone.

When the mob tore you, you were doubly torn:
Once for yourself, once for your art.
You were mistaken, Cinna, to be born.

Triple Guard

Those who are fond of knocking off marble
fingers and more than fingers here confront
unknockable bronze.

He can defend himself, this youth.
Beyond and within his superhuman hardness
his fists are ready.

And something more—being too calm
too perfect not to rebuff (while he allures)
the plundering eye.

Irreproachable, unapproachable,
self-contained and safe for a long time yet,
a long time yet.

Able

Both to converse and to conserve
Frugal and fruitful, passionate-patient

Never mistaking facility for felicity
Salesmanship for craftsmanship

Skeptical of commendation or condemnation
This is the man.

My Teachers Are the Centripetal Ones

The dervish turning in one timeless spot;
The thinker focusing the lens of thought;

The scholar in his self-convicted cell;
The saint God-centered and centripetal;

The watcher whose long motionlessness matches
The insect stillness of the thing he watches;

The marksman whose curled finger waits to move;
The lover, absent, aiming on his love.

Museum Vase
For W. A.

It contains nothing.
We ask it
To contain nothing.

Having transcended use
It is endlessly
Content to be.

Still it broods
On old burdens—
Wheat, oil, wine.

Skier

He swings down like the flourish of a pen
Signing a signature in white on white.

The silence of his skis reciprocates
The silence of the world around him.

Wind is his one competitor
In the cool winding and unwinding down.

On incandescent feet he falls
Unfalling, trailing white foam, white fire.

Metal and Mettle

The slow laborer and the speedy athlete
it would be hard to choose between
for the esthetic satisfaction of watching.

One bronze back is pushing
a wheelbarrow level with cement up
an inclined gangplank steadily

the center line of the back undulating
at each step like a cobra delicately
dancing to the flute.

Metal for hardness, for sheen, for
durability but for man the word is mettle
a variant of metal.

What does the athlete finally have?
At best a victory but the laborer
has a new building, a building built.

Riddler

He comes out as a brook comes out of snow
From no identifiable address,
And you nor I nor anyone else can guess
Where he is going, where he is going to go.

His name is Huckleberry, alias John.
He'll sail you (if he had it) any craft
Such as a Mississippi-going raft
And when the big waves hit him, he'll hang on.

Gun-metal water with a gleam of sun
Matches his eye but not his devil-may-care.
He leaps from silence into shout to dare
What anyone else has done, or hasn't done.

Always a trace of riddle on his lips
Curled half in amity, half in defiance.
Jack-the-Giant-Killer (given the giants)—
He is the boy who stows away on ships.

In Memoriam: Four Poets

I

Searock his tower above the sea,
Searock he built, not ivory.
Searock as well his haunted art
Who gave to plunging hawks his heart.

II

He loved to stand upon his head
To demonstrate he was not dead.
Ah, if his poems misbehave
'Tis only to defy the grave.

III

This exquisite patrician bird
Grooming a neatly folded wing
Guarded for years the Sacred Word.
A while he sang then ceased to sing.

IV

His head carved out of granite O,
His hair a wayward drift of snow,
He worshipped the great God of Flow
By holding on and letting go.

Enviable

Enviable, not envious, the little worm
Whose apple is his world and equally his home,
Who at his feasting hears no hint of doom.

Deep, deep in love he is, who could be deeper in?
He envies no one, he could envy whom?
I envy no one, I could envy him.

Condor

How flawless and unvarying his candor
Over the wide, over the high Andes
The great condor

So infinitely far from all dissembling.
Is there a doubt? He dares, he dares the sun
To watch him

And the sun watches. Watches, watches the condor
Over the wide, over the high Andes
With equal candor.

Astronomer

Far far
Beyond the stargazer
The astronomer

Who does not try
To make the sky
His sky

But goes out of his mind
To find
Beyond.

Nightly he goes
Nightly he knows
Where no comfort is

And this
His comfort is
His irreducible peace.

Uncanny traveler
To leave himself how far
Behind.

Eagle Soaring

Only in the perfection of his calligraphy
With its classic loops and severe flourishes,
The scribe inseparable from his inscription,
The writer and the writing one, moving
As slowly as a slowed moving picture—

Only in the strict dance, the passacaglia
Endlessly repeating endless variation,
Grave as a ceremonial saraband
For which the clouds are choreographers,
The wings taut with formality and formal ease—

Above all in the complete undistraction
And extreme loneliness of his observational
From which he bows and broods on the round world,
Turning as if in imitation of her turning,
Obedient to nothing but the pure act of seeing—

Siege

Indian-wise
We have kept moving in
With slant leaf-eyes
At windows room by room.
Your window-light is a light gloom now.
Isn't this what you wanted?

You've let us come, have watched us come
Until with any wind at all
Our hands brush on the outer wall
And brush again.
Your house is shadow-haunted.

You've let us come—
Give us a few years more
We'll undertake to bar and bind your door
To keep you always and forever home.
Isn't this what you wanted?

Come

As you are (said Death)
Come green, come gray, come white
Bring nothing at all
Unless it's a perfectly easy
Petal or two of snow
Perhaps or a daisy
Come day, come night.

Nothing fancy now
No rose, no evening star
Come spring, come fall
Nothing but a blade of rain
Come gray, come green
As you are (said Death)
As you are.

"Paper Men to Air Hopes and Fears"

The first speaker said
Fear fire. Fear furnaces
Incinerators, the city dump
The faint scratch of match.

The second speaker said
Fear water. Fear drenching rain
Drizzle, oceans, puddles, a damp
Day and the flush toilet.

The third speaker said
Fear wind. And it needn't be
A hurricane. Drafts, open
Windows, electric fans.

The fourth speaker said
Fear knives. Fear any sharp
Thing, machine, shears
Scissors, lawnmowers.

The fifth speaker said
Hope. Hope for the best
A smooth folder in a steel file.

POEMS
1950-1960

Sailboat, Your Secret

Sailboat, your secret. With what dove-and-serpent
Craft you trick the old antagonist.
Trick and transpose, snaring him into sponsor.

The blusterer—his blows you twist to blessing.
Your tactics and your tact, O subtle one,
Your war, your peace—you who defer and win.

Not in obeisance, not in defiance you bow,
You bow to him, but in deep irony.
The gull's wing kisses the whitecap not more archly

Than yours. Timeless and motionless I watch
Your craftsmanship, your wiles, O skimmer-schemer,
Your losses to profit, your wayward onwardness.

Apple Peeler

Why the unbroken spiral, Virtuoso,
Like a trick sonnet in one long, versatile sentence?

Is it a pastime merely, this perfection,
For an old man, sharp knife, long night, long winter?

Or do your careful fingers move at the stir
Of unadmitted immemorial magic?

Solitaire. The ticking clock. The apple
Turning, turning as the round earth turns.

High Diver

How deep is his duplicity who in a flash
Passes from resting bird to flying bird to fish,

Who momentarily is sculpture, then all motion,
Speed and splash, then climbs again to contemplation.

He is the archer who himself is bow and arrow.
He is the upper-under-world-commuting hero.

His downward going has the air of sacrifice
To some dark seaweed-bearded seagod face to face.

Or goddess. Rippling and responsive lies the water
For him to contemplate, then powerfully to enter.

Monadnock

If to the taunting peneplain the peak
Is standpat, relic, anachronism,
Fossil, the peak can stand the taunt.

There was a time the peak was not a peak
But granite and resistant core,
Something that refused to wear

Away when time and wind and rivers wore
The rest away. Here is the thing
The nervous rivers left behind.

Endurance is the word, not exaltation.
Two words: endurance, exaltation.
Out of endurance, exaltation.

The Orb Weaver

Here is the spinner, the orb weaver,
Devised of jet, embossed with sulphur,
Hanging among the fruits of summer,

Hour after hour serenely sullen,
Ripening as September ripens,
Plumping like a grape or melon.

And in its winding-sheet the grasshopper.

The art, the craftsmanship, the cunning,
The patience, the self-control, the waiting,
The sudden dart and the needled poison.

I have no quarrel with the spider
But with the mind or mood that made her
To thrive in nature and in man's nature.

Swimmer

I

Observe how he negotiates his way
With trust and the least violence, making
The stranger friend, the enemy ally.
The depth that could destroy gently supports him.
With water he defends himself from water.
Danger he leans on, rests in. The drowning sea
Is all he has between himself and drowning.

II

What lover ever lay more mutually
With his beloved, his always-reaching arms
Stroking in smooth and powerful caresses?
Some drown in love as in dark water, and some
By love are strongly held as the green sea
Now holds the swimmer. Indolently he turns
To float. The swimmer floats, the lover sleeps.

Sun

Arch-democrat of our enlightenment,
More Jeffersonian than Jefferson,
You warm and warn us with your declaration,
You dazzle us noonly with your rights of man.

Impartially and with strict indifference
You span, cross, and belittle rivers and ranges
And every boundary natural and unnatural
And every visible or invisible fence.

Your light—unspeculated in, unhoarded,
Unallocated, unrationed, and untaxed,
Unprocessed, unpackaged, and unsold—affirms
Uneconomic unpolitical fact.

Your being or non-being philosophers
Do not dispute. *You* are your evidence.
And the simple do not have to have revealed
To them, Revealer, your benevolence.

The loved, the unloved, indistinguishably,
Lift to your comprehensive kiss. Where
Could be rival constancy-intensity?
Where else so gentle and so fierce a fire?

O Sun, unbribed, unbribable and pure,
Sun irreproachable, juster and more
Equitable than jury, judge, and court,
You guarantee the basest weed its light.

Under your blaze grass greens and flowers glitter,
The white sheet on the line burns whiter, whiter,
To terra cotta the slow sun bather tempers
And the pouring water-bather turns pure copper.

Waxwings

Four Tao philosophers as cedar waxwings
chat on a February berrybush
in sun, and I am one.

Such merriment and such sobriety—
the small wild fruit on the tall stalk—
was this not always my true style?

Above an elegance of snow, beneath
a silk-blue sky a brotherhood of four
birds. Can you mistake us?

To sun, to feast, and to converse
and all together—for this I have abandoned
all my other lives.

O World of Toms

O world of Toms—tomfools, Tom Peppers,
Dark Peeping Toms and Tom-the-Pipers,
Tom Paines, Tom Joneses, Tom Aquinases,
Undoubting Toms and Doubting Thomases,
Tomboys, Tom Thumbs, Tom-Dick-and-Harries,
Tom Collinses and Tom-and-Jerries,
Tom Wolfes, Tom Jeffersons, Tom Hardies,
Tom cods, tomcats, tomtits, tom-turkeys—
O hospitable world! And still they come
In every shape and shade of Tom.

Hallelujah: A Sestina

A wind's word, the Hebrew Hallelujah.
I wonder they never give it to a boy
(Hal for short) boy with wind-wild hair.
It means Praise God, as well it should since praise
Is what God's for. Why didn't they call my father
Hallelujah instead of Ebenezer?

Eben, of course, but christened Ebenezer,
Product of Nova Scotia (hallelujah).
Daniel, a country doctor, was his father
And my father his tenth and final boy.
A baby and last, he had a baby's praise:
Red petticoat, red cheeks, and crow-black hair.

A boy has little say about his hair
And little about a name like Ebenezer
Except that he can shorten either. Praise
God for that, for that shout Hallelujah.
Shout Hallelujah for everything a boy
Can be that is not his father or grandfather.

But then, before you know it, he is a father
Too and passing on his brand of hair
To one more perfectly defenceless boy,
Dubbing him John or James or Ebenezer
But never, so far as I know, Hallelujah,
As if God didn't need quite that much praise.

But what I'm coming to — Could I ever praise
My father half enough for being a father
Who let me be myself? Sing Hallelujah.
Preacher he was with a prophet's head of hair
And what but a prophet's name was Ebenezer,
However little I guessed it as a boy?

Outlandish names of course are never a boy's
Choice. And it takes time to learn to praise.
Stone of Help is the meaning of Ebenezer.
Stone of Help—what fitter name for my father?
Always the Stone of Help however his hair
Might graduate from black to Hallelujah.

Such is the old drama of boy and father.
Praise from a grayhead now with thinning hair.
Sing Ebenezer, Robert, sing Hallelujah!

Boy Riding Forward Backward

Presto, pronto! Two boys, two horses.
But the boy on backward riding forward
Is the boy to watch.

He rides the forward horse and laughs
In the face of the forward boy on the backward
Horse, and *he* laughs

Back and the horses laugh. They gallop.
The trick is the cool barefaced pretense
There is no trick.

They might be flying, face to face,
On a fast train. They might be whitecaps
Hot-cool-headed,

One curling backward, one curving forward,
Racing a rivalry of waves.
They might, they might—

Across a blue of lake, through trees,
And half a mile away I caught them:
Two boys, two horses.

Through trees and through binoculars
Sweeping for birds. Oh, they were birds
All right, all right,

Swallows that weave and wave and sweep
And skim and swoop and skitter until
The last trees take them.

Farm Boy After Summer

A seated statue of himself he seems.
A bronze slowness becomes him. Patently
The page he contemplates he doesn't see.

The lesson, the long lesson, has been summer.
His mind holds summer as his skin holds sun.
For once the homework, all of it, was done.

What were the crops, where were the fiery fields
Where for so many days so many hours
The sun assaulted him with glittering showers?

Expect a certain absence in his presence.
Expect all winter long a summer scholar,
For scarcely all its snows can cool that color.

The Hawk

Who is the hawk whose squeal
Is like the shivering sound
Of a too tightly wound
Child's toy that slips a reel?

But beyond who is why.
Why any cry at all
Since death knows how to fall
Soundlessly from the sky?

Three Darks Come Down Together

Three darks come down together,
Three darks close in around me:
Day dark, year dark, dark weather.

They whisper and conspire,
They search me and they sound me
Hugging my private fire.

Day done, year done, storm blowing,
Three darknesses impound me
With dark of white snow snowing.

Three darks gang up to end me,
To browbeat and dumbfound me.
Three future lights defend me.

Cypresses

At noon they talk of evening and at evening
Of night, but what they say at night
Is a dark secret.

Somebody long ago called them the Trees
Of Death and they have never forgotten.
The name enchants them.

Always an attitude of solitude
To point the paradox of standing
Alone together.

How many years they have been teaching birds
In little schools, by little skills,
How to be shadows.

Gold

Suddenly all the gold I ever wanted
Let loose and fell on me. A storm of gold
Starting with rain a quick sun catches falling
And in the rain (fall within fall) a whirl
Of yellow leaves, glitter of paper nuggets.

And there were puddles the sun was winking at
And fountains saucy with goldfish, fantails, sunfish,
And trout slipping in streams it would be insult
To call gold and, trailing their incandescent
Fingers, meteors and a swimming moon.

Flowers of course. Chrysanthemums and clouds
Of twisted cool witch hazel and marigolds,
Late dandelions and all the goldenrods.
And bees all pollen and honey, wasps gold-banded
And hornets dangling their legs, cruising the sun.

The luminous birds, goldfinches and orioles,
Were gone or going, leaving some of their gold
Behind in near-gold, off-gold, ultra-golden
Beeches, birches, maples, apples. And under
The appletrees the lost, the long-lost names.

Pumpkins and squashes heaped in a cold-gold sunset—
Oh, I was crushed like Croesus, Midas-smothered
And I died in a maple-fall a boy was raking
Nightward to burst all bonfire-gold together—
And leave at last in a thin blue prayer of smoke.

Glass

Words of a poem should be glass
But glass so simple-subtle its shape
Is nothing but the shape of what it holds.

A glass spun for itself is empty,
Brittle, at best Venetian trinket.
Embossed glass hides the poem or its absence.

Words should be looked through, should be windows.
The best word were invisible.
The poem is the thing the poet thinks.

If the impossible were not
And if the glass, only the glass,
Could be removed, the poem would remain.

Tomatoes

Nature and God by some elusive yet felicitous
Division of labor that I do not comprehend
(Salts of the soil, rain, the exuberant August sun,
Omniscience, omnipresence, and omnipotence)
Contrived these gaudy fruits, but I was the gardener
And in their lustihood, their hot vermilion luster,
Their unassailable three-dimensionality,
Their unashamed fatness, share the glory and fulfillment.

Now while the sacrificial knife is in abeyance
They bask and blaze serenely on the sun-splashed sill
For the last perfection of ripeness. A thank offering.
A peace offering. A still life. So still, so lifelike
The fruit becomes the painted picture of the fruit.

Ritual

Night comes no wilier inch-wise step-wise
shadow by shadow, tree by tree,
than at the edge of night, single,
and with exquisite circumspection,
the ruffed grouse.

She has evaded, O how she
evades, the wildfire fox, the hound,
the fowler's snare, the harrier sun,
the moon's cold machinations and
the great eared owl.

Masked and peripheral, she waits,
tingling with intimations, for one
more overtone of darkness against
her ritual supper on the snow:
the small gold maize.

Bluejay

So bandit-eyed, so undovelike a bird
to be my pastoral father's favorite—
skulker and blusterer
whose every arrival is a raid.

Love made the bird no gentler
nor him who loved less gentle.
Still, still the wild blue feather
brings my mild father.

Dog-Day Night

Just before night darkens to total night
A child at the next farm is calling, calling,
Calling her dog. Heat and the death of wind
Bring the small wailing like a mosquito close.
Will nothing stop her? Yet my complaining adds
To my complaint. Welcome it like a bird,
A whippoorwill, I say, closing my windows
North and east. The voice evades the glass.
She will not, will not let the dog be lost.
Why don't they tell her, isn't she old enough
To hear how the whole dog-gone earth is loose
And snooping through the dark and won't come home?

The Spy

To leave his empty house yet not to leave it
But make himself a shadow at a window—
Who is this prowler private in the moonlight?

Then at another window and another,
His face against the glass and peering in—
What does he think he sees or wants to see?

Soft as the milkweed floss the September night.
White as the milkweed the untroubled moon
Whose face, though far, is also at the window.

Two faces, but the prowler peers in deeper
Spying upon the empty chair, spying
Upon the man who is and is not there.

Floruit

Daringly, yet how unerringly
They bring to the cool and nun-like virtues
Of patience or something older than patience,
Silence, absolute silence, and obedience
All the hot virtues of the sun
And being wholly sex are wholly pure.

If with an equal candor we could face
Their unguarded faces, if we could look in silence
Long enough, could we touch finally,
We who when luckiest are said to flower,
Their fiery innocence, their day-long unabashed
Fulfillment, their unregretful falling?

Hide-and-Seek

Here where the dead lie hidden
Too well ever to speak,
Three children unforbidden
Are playing hide-and-seek.

What if for such a hiding
These stones were not designed?
The dead are far from chiding;
The living need not mind.

Too soon the stones that hid them
Anonymously in play
Will learn their names and bid them
Come back to hide to stay.

The Rock Climbers

In this soft age, in my soft
middle age, the rock climbers

Who giving all to love
embrace cold cliffs

Or with spread-eagle arms
enact a crucifixion

Hanging between the falling
and the not-attaining

Observed or unobserved
by hawks and vultures—

How vaulting a humility
superb a supererogation

Craggy to break the mind
on and to cool the mind.

Two Bums Walk Out of Eden

Two bums walk out of Eden. Evening approaches
The suave, the decorous trees, the careful grass,
The strict green benches—and the two bums go.

They caught the official nod, the backward-pointing
Thumb, and now they rise and leave a little
Briskly as men heedful to waste no time—

As men bending their steps toward due appointments.
The tall one looms like a skeleton; the runt
Walks with the totter of a tumbleweed.

Down the trimmed ceremonial path they go
Together, silent and separate and eyes
Ahead like soldiers. Down the long path and out.

What desert blanched these faces? What blowing sands
Gullied the eyes and wrecked the hanging hands
While Babylon and Nineveh were falling?

Now a shade darker will be a shade less dark.
Now there is room for evening in the park
Where cool episcopal bells are calling, calling.

Cold

Cold and the colors of cold: mineral, shell,
And burning blue. The sky is on fire with blue
And wind keeps ringing, ringing the fire bell.

I am caught up into a chill as high
As creaking glaciers and powder-plumed peaks
And the absolutes of interstellar sky.

Abstract, impersonal, metaphysical, pure,
This dazzling art derides me. How should warm breath
Dare to exist—exist, exult, endure?

Hums in my ear the old Ur-father of freeze
And burn, that pre-post-Christian Fellow before
And after all myths and demonologies.

Under the glaring and sardonic sun,
Behind the icicles and double glass
I huddle, hoard, hold out, hold on, hold on.

Desiring to Give All

Desiring to give all, to be all gift,
A living giver, then a giver dead,
He gave to friends the liveliness of his head,
Then stretching generosity with thrift,
Pondered if head itself, the clean bare skull,
Might not be saved and deeded to a friend
So that memorial and functional
Might thrive and blend
In an undying fate
As doorstop or as paperweight.

Burial

Aloft, lightly on fingertips
As crewmen carry a racing shell—
But I was lighter than any shell or ship.

An easy trophy, they picked me up and bore me,
Four of them, an even four.
I knew the pulse and impulse of those hands,

And heard the talking, laughing. I heard
As from an adjoining room, the door ajar,
Voices but not words.

If I am dead (I said)
If this is death,
How casual, how delicate its masque and myth.

One pallbearer, the tenor, spoke,
Another whistled softly, and I tried to smile.
Death? Music? Or a joke?

But still the hands were there.
I rode half on the hands and half in air.
Their strength was equal to my strangeness.

Whatever they do (I said) will be done right,
Whether in earth and dark or in deep light,
Whatever the hands do will be well.

Suddenly I tried to breathe and cry:
Before you put me down, before
I finally die,

Take from the filing folders of my brain
All that is finished or begun—
Then I remembered that this had been done.

So we went on, on
To our party-parting on the hill
Of the blue breath, gray boulders, and my burial.

The Seed Eaters

The seed eaters, the vegetarian birds,
Redpolls, grosbeaks, crossbills, finches, siskins,
Fly south to winter in our north, so making
A sort of Florida of our best blizzards.

Weed seeds and seeds of pine cones are their pillage,
Alder and birch catkins, such vegetable
Odds and ends as the winged keys of maple
As well as roadside sumac, red-plush-seeded.

Hi! with a bounce in snowflake flocks come juncos
As if a hand had flipped them and tree sparrows,
Now nip and tuck and playing tag, now squatting
All weather-proofed and feather-fluffed on snow.

Hard fare, full feast, I'll say, deep cold, high spirits.
Here's Christmas to Candlemas on a bunting's budget.
From this old seed eater with his beans, his soybeans,
Cracked corn, cracked wheat, peanuts and split peas, hail!

Demonstration

With what economy, what indolent control
The hawk lies on the delicate air, looking below.
He does not climb—watch him—he does not need to climb.

The same invisible shaft that lifts the cumulus
Lifts him, lifts him to any altitude he wills.
Never his wings, only his scream, disturbs noon stillness.

Days of the sharp-cut cloud, mid-day, he demonstrates
Over and ever again the spiral. On smooth blue ice
Impeccable the figure-skater carves his curves.

Oh, how to separate (inseparable in the bird)
His altitude from his incessant livelihood:
His higher mathematics, his hunger on the ground.

Weathervane

Moving unmoved
Like the fixed tree
For constancy
But like the leaf
Aware
Of all the tricks
And politics
Of air.

Fickle?
Let the fool laugh
Who fails to see
That only he
Who freely turns
Discerns,
Moving unmoved
Is free.

Come Out Into the Sun

Come out into the sun and bathe your eyes
In undiluted light. On the old brass
Of winter-tarnished grass,
Under these few bronze leaves of oak
Suspended, and a blue ghost of chimney smoke
Sit and grow wise
And empty as a simpleton.

The meadow mouse twitching her nose in prayer
Sniffs at a sunbeam like celestial cheese.
Come out, come out into the sun
And bask your knees
And be an acolyte of the illumined air.
The weathercock who yesterday was cold
Today sings hallelujah hymns in gold.

Soon the small snake will slip her skin
And the gray moth in an old ritual
Unseal her silk cocoon.
Come shed, shed now, your winter-varnished shell
In the deep diathermy of high noon.
The sun, the sun, come out into the sun,
Into the sun, come out, come in.

Epitaph

Believer he and unbeliever both
For less than both would have been less than truth.
His creed was godliness and godlessness.
His credit had been cramped with any less.

Freedom he loved and order he embraced.
Fifty extremists called him Janus-faced.
Though cool centrality was his desire,
He drew the zealot fire and counter-fire.

Baffled by what he deeply understood,
He found life evil and he found life good.
Lover he was, unlonely, yet alone—
Esteemed, belittled, nicknamed, and unknown.

Thistle Seed in the Wind

Pioneer, paratrooper, missionary of the gospel seed,
Discoverer, skylarker, parable of solitude,
Where is the mathematics, wisp, to tell your chance?
If when you fall you fail,
Are lost at last and die,
At least you will have made the great voyage out,
Your sun-saluting sail alone on the blue ocean-sky.
Hail, voyager, hail!

The Disengaging Eagle

There is a rumor
    the eagle tires of being eagle
    and would change wing
    with a less kingly bird as king,
    say, the seagull.

    With swans and cranes and geese,
    so the rumor goes,
    finding his official pose
    faintly absurd,
    he would aspire to unofficial peace
    and be, if possible, pure bird.

There is a rumor
    the eagle nurses now a mood
    to abdicate
    forever and for good
    as flagpole-sitter for the State.

    Is it the fall of age
    merely, a geriatrical complaint,
    this drift to disengage,
    this cool unrage?
    or rather some dark philosophic taint?

There is a rumor
    (God save us) the old warrior
    who screamed against the sun
    and toured with Caesar and Napoleon
    cavils now at war

    and would allegedly retire,
    resign, retreat
    to a blue solitude,
    an inaccessible country seat
    to fan a native fire,
    a purely personal feud.

EARLIER
POEMS

Seagulls

Between the under and the upper blue
All day the seagulls climb and swerve and soar,
Arc intersecting arc, curve over curve.

And you may watch them weaving a long time
And never see their pattern twice the same
And never see their pattern once imperfect.

Take any moment they are in the air—
If you could change them, if you had the power
How would you place them other than they are?

What we have labored all our lives to have
And failed, these birds effortlessly achieve:
Freedom that flows in form and still is free.

Serpent as Vine

Once I observed a serpent climb a tree.
Just once. It went up twisting like a vine,
Around, around, then out across a branch,
And though it went up faster than a vine,
It did not seem to hurry as it went.

And having reached a certain bough, it lay
As quiet as a vine. I could not tell
Its secret there among the summer leaves.
But what I knew I knew exceeding well:
That something underfoot was overhead.

True North

The needle has its north but not true north
For its direction
Wanders and constantly requires correction.

Nor is the star whose name is north true north
Though it turns near
The pole of the celestial hemisphere.

Nothing that we can follow is true north,
Nothing we see,
Being a point in pure geometry.

And even—so I understand—true north
Does not stay true
But slowly travels in a circle too.

Perhaps it would be true to say true north
Does not exist
Except to the extreme idealist.

But for all ordinary needs of north
Compass and star
Are north enough to guide the mariner.

Interrupted Fern

Interrupted fern we call it
As if design for reproduction
Were nothing but an imperfection.
As if we disapproved the function.
As if of all the ferns and bracken
This were the faulty and mistaken.
As if the fern called for correction—
The fern and not our empty fiction,
The fern and not our clumsy diction.
Henceforth I take this fern as token
Of all things fertile, whole, unbroken.

The Wasp

As I was reading, a wasp lit on the page
Whose burden was that man knows nothing, nothing,
And slowly walked across. And at the edge

It paused to reconsider. I paused too.
I took it for a marginal annotation.
I let the text go and I read the wasp.

Or rather say, I tried to read the wasp.
I turned the book this way and that the way
A child might try a Greek word upside down.

I counted feelers, wings, and legs, for letters.
I looked it in the eye but could not tell
Whether for certain it returned my look.

Perhaps the gist of what the side-note said
Was that a wasp could read the printed word
As well as man could read the total world.

Or else the meaning may have been that man,
If he knows nothing, knows that he knows nothing,
Whereas the wasp knows only what it knows.

Blue Winter

Winter uses all the blues there are.
One shade of blue for water, one for ice,
Another blue for shadows over snow.
The clear or cloudy sky uses blue twice—
Both different blues. And hills row after row
Are colored blue according to how far.
You know the bluejay's double-blue device
Shows best when there are no green leaves to show.
And Sirius is a winterbluegreen star.

The Sound I Listened For

What I remember is the ebb and flow of sound
That summer morning as the mower came and went
And came again, crescendo and diminuendo,
And always when the sound was loudest how it ceased
A moment while he backed the horses for the turn,
The rapid clatter giving place to the slow click
And the mower's voice. That was the sound I listened for.
The voice did what the horses did. It shared the action
As sympathetic magic does or incantation.
The voice hauled and the horses hauled. The strength of one
Was in the other and in the strength was no impatience.
Over and over as the mower made his rounds
I heard his voice and only once or twice he backed
And turned and went ahead and spoke no word at all.

The Old of the Moon in August

"The old of the moon in August," the old man said,
"Is the time to cut your brush. You cut it then
You won't be having to cut if off again."

I judge he meant the dead that month stay dead.
I must remember—August, the August moon,
The old of the moon, the old of the moon. Amen.

As Near To Eden

Hearing the cry I looked to see a bird
Among the boughs that overhung the stream.
No bird was there. The cry was not a bird's.
Then I looked down and saw the snake and saw
The frog. Half of the frog was free to cry.
The other half the snake had in its jaws.
The snake was silent as the sand it lay on.

I ran to blast the thing out of my sight,
But the snake ran first (untouched) into the water
Fluid to fluid and so disappeared
And all I saw and heard was flowing water.

I dipped a foot in slowly and began
To saunter down the stream a little way
As I had done so many times before
That summer. Now I went more cautiously
Watching the water every step, but water
Had washed the thing away and washed it clean.

Over the stream I had a kind of bed
Built of an old smooth board and four large stones
And there between the sun and water I
Would often spend an early afternoon.
It was as near to Eden as I knew—
This alternating cool and warm, this blend
Of cool and warm, of water-song and silence.
No one could see me there and even insects
Left me alone.
        I turned upon my face
And so had darkness for my eyes and fire
On my back. I felt my breathing slacken, deepen.
After a time I reached a hand over
And let the fingertips trail in the water.

Strange, strange that in a world so old and rich
In good and evil, the death (or all but death)
Of one inconsequential squealing frog
Should have concerned me so, should for the moment
Have seemed the only evil in the world
And overcoming it the only good.

But they were symbols too, weren't they? the frog,
The snake? The frog of course being innocence
Sitting with golden and unwinking eyes
Hour after hour beside a waterweed
As rapt and meditative as a saint
Beneath a palm tree, and the snake being—well,
That's all been told before.
                                        A pretty contrast,
Yet even under the indulgent sun
And half asleep I knew my picture false.
The frog was no more innocent than the snake
And if he looked the saint he was a fake.
He and the snake were all too closely kin,
First cousins once removed under the skin.
If snakes ate frogs, frogs in their turn ate flies
And both could look ridiculously wise.
But neither one knew how to feed on lies
As man could do—that is, philosophize.
And having reached that point I closed my eyes,
Rhyming myself and sunning myself to sleep.

And while I slept my body was a sundial
Casting its moving, slowly moving shadow
Across the moving, swiftly moving water.

When I awoke I had one clear desire:
The coolness of that swiftly moving water.

Yet still I waited, it was so near, so sure,
The superfluity of heat so good.

And then I sat straight up having heard a sound
I recognized too well. It was no bird.
Slipping and splashing as I went I ran
Upstream. I couldn't see, I didn't need
To see to know. So all the time I'd slept
And sunned myself and entertained myself
With symbolizing and unsymbolizing
Good and evil, *this* had been going on.

They were hidden now among the roots of a tree
The stream had washed the soil from. I found a stick
And jabbed it in as far as I could reach
Again and again until I broke the stick.
But still I kept it up until the snake
Having disgorged slipped out and got away.
And still I kept it up until the frog
Must have been pulp and ground into the sand.
The stick, all that was left, I threw as far
As I could throw.
               Then I went home and dressed.
Eden was done for for one day at least.

Sheep

From where I stand the sheep stand still
As stones against the stony hill.

The stones are gray
And so are they.

And both are weatherworn and round,
Leading the eye back to the ground.

Two mingled flocks—
The sheep, the rocks.

And still no sheep stirs from its place
Or lifts its Babylonian face.

Two Women

November seemed to haunt the place.
The house was colorless as rain.
Two women standing face to face
Were polishing a windowpane.

One looked outdoors, the other in.
One had white hair, the other gray.
One saw herself as she had been,
The other saw the other way.

They moved white cloths against the glass.
The glass was all there was between.
They did not pause to watch me pass
Or let me see that I was seen.

The clouds above the house were white,
The trees were green, the sky was blue,
And birds in sky and trees were bright,
But that was all that summer could do.

I Am Not Flattered

I am not flattered that a bell
About the neck of a peaceful cow
Should be more damning to my ear
Than all the bombing planes of hell
Merely because the bell is near,
Merely because the bell is now,
The bombs too far away to hear.

Good Night Near Christmas

And now good night. Good night to this old house
Whose breathing fires are banked for their night's rest.
Good night to lighted windows in the west.
Good night to neighbors and to neighbors' cows

Whose morning milk will be beside my door.
Good night to one star shining in. Good night
To earth, poor earth with its uncertain light,
Our little wandering planet still at war.

Good night to one unstarved and gnawing mouse
Between the inner and the outer wall.
He has a paper nest in which to crawl.
Good night to men who have no bed, no house.

Sing a Song of Juniper

Sing a song of juniper
Whose song is seldom sung,
Whose needles prick the finger,
Whose berries burn the tongue.

Sing a song of juniper
With boughs shaped like a bowl
For holding sun or snowfall
High on the pasture knoll.

Sing a song of juniper
Whose green is more than green,
Is blue and bronze and violet
And colors in between.

Sing a song of juniper
That keeps close to the ground,
A song composed of silence
And very little sound.

Sing a song of juniper
That hides the hunted mouse,
And gives me outdoor shadows
To haunt my indoor house.

Invitation

You who have meant to come, come now
With strangeness on the morning snow
Before the early morning plow
Makes half the snowy strangeness go.

You who have meant to come, come now
When only *your* footprints will show,
Before one overburdened bough
Spills snow above on snow below.

You who were meant to come, come now.
If you were meant to come, you'll know.

Juniper

From where I live, from windows on four sides
I see four common kinds of evergreen:
White pine, pitch pine, cedar, and juniper.
The last is less than tree. It hugs the ground.
It would be last for any wind to break
If wind could break the others. Pines would go first
As some of them have gone, and cedars next,
Though where is wind to blow a cedar down?
To overthrow a juniper a wind
Would have to blow the ground away beneath it.

Not wind but fire. I heard a farmer say
One lighted match dropped on a juniper
Would do the trick. And he had done the trick.
I try to picture how it would look: thin snow
Over the pasture and dark junipers
Over the snow and darker for the snow,
Each juniper swirl-shaped like flame itself.
Then from the slow green fire the swift hot fire
Flares, sputters with resin, roars, dies
While the next juniper goes next.
                                        Poets
Are rich in points of view if they are rich
In anything. The farmer thinks one thing;
The poet can afford to think all things
Including what the farmer thinks, thinking
Around the farmer rather than above him,
Loving the evergreen the farmer hates,
And yet not hating him for hating it.

I know another fire in juniper,
Have felt its heat burn on my back, have breathed
Its invisible smoke, climbing New England hills
In summer. Have known the concentrated sun

Of hard blue berries, chewed them, and spit them out,
Their juice burning my throat. Juniper.

Its colors are the metals: tarnished bronze
And copper, violet of tarnished silver,
And if you turn it, white aluminum.
So many colors in so dull a green
And I so many years before I saw them.

I see those colors now, and far, far more
Than color. I see all that we have in common
Here where we live together on this hill.
And what I hope for is for more in common.

Here is my faith, my vision, my burning bush.
It will burn on and never be consumed.
It will be here long after I have gone,
Long after the last farmer sleeps. And since
I speak for it, its silence speaks for me.

Artist

He cuts each log in lengths exact
As truly as truth cuts a fact.

When he has sawed an honest pile
Of wood, he stops and chops awhile.

Each section is twice split in two
As truly as a fact is true.

Then having split all to be split,
He sets to work at stacking it.

No comb constructed by a bee
Is more a work of symmetry

Than is this woodstack whose strict grace
Is having each piece in its place.

The Mouse Whose Name is Time

The mouse whose name is Time
Is out of sound and sight.
He nibbles at the day
And nibbles at the night.

He nibbles at the summer
Till all of it is gone.
He nibbles at the seashore.
He nibbles at the moon.

Yet no man not a seer,
No woman not a sibyl
Can ever ever hear
Or see him nibble, nibble.

And whence or how he comes
And how or where he goes
Nobody dead remembers,
Nobody living knows.

Indoor Lady

An indoor lady whom I know
Laments the lateness of the spring—
The sun, the birds, the buds so slow,
The superannuated snow,
The wind that is possessed to blow.

Her sadly window-watching eyes,
Her uttered and unuttered sighs
For such unseasonable skies
Give me to understand that spring
In other years was otherwise.

Night Train

Across the dim frozen fields of night
Where is it going, where is it going?
No throb of wheels, no rush of light,
Only a whistle blowing, blowing,
Only a whistle blowing.

Something echoing through my brain,
Something timed between sleep and waking,
Murmurs, murmurs this may be the train
I must be sometime, somewhere taking,
I must be sometime taking.

Shelley

Each had her claim.
To each he gave consent:
To water, his liquid name,
His burning body to flame,
To earth the sediment
And the snatched heart, his fame
To the four winds. He went
As severally as he came—
Element to element.
Each had her claim.

Comet

The comet comes again.
Astronomer, tell when.

When ends its long eclipse?
Where meets the long ellipse?

Plot its explicit path
In geometric graph.

Trace its eccentric course
Through the curved universe.

Expound to us the law
By which we see again
The comet we first saw
As boys, now as old men.

Statement

I follow Plato only with my mind.
Pure beauty strikes me as a little thin,
A little cold, however beautiful.

I am in love with what is mixed, impure,
Doubtful and dark and hard to disencumber.
I want a beauty I must dig for, search for.

Pure beauty is beginning and not end.
Begin with sun and drop from sun to cloud,
From cloud to tree, from tree to earth itself,

And deeper yet down to the earth-dark root.
I am in love with what resists my loving,
With what I have to labor to make live.

As Easily as Trees

As easily as trees have dropped
Their leaves, so easily a man,
So unreluctantly, might drop
All rags, ambitions, and regrets
Today and lie with leaves in sun.
So he might sleep while they began,
Falling or blown, to cover him.

The Two Uses

The eye is not more exquisitely designed
For seeing than it is for being loved.
The same lips curved to speak are curved to kiss.
Even the workaday and practical arm
Becomes all love for love's sake to the lover.

If this is nature's thrift, love thrives on it.
Love never asks the body different
Or ever wants it less ambiguous,
The eye being lovelier for what it sees,
The arm for all it does, the lips for speaking.

Simple Death

It is a little thing to die.
A little thing it is to lie
Down on a common bed and die.
There need be no wide watchful sky
To watch one die, nor human eye.
No inauspicious bird need cry
At death nor flying need it fly
Otherwise than birds fly
Whether or not some man will die.
No man about to die need try
To die or wonder how or why
Or say a prayer or say good-bye
Or even know that he will die.

White Sunday Morning

White Sunday morning long ago—
White bedroom curtains and white walls,
Beyond the window falling snow
That dillydallies as it falls,
And in the kitchen down below
An old old woman popping corn,
Popping corn on Sunday morning.
Thanks to the little register
Cut in my floor above her stove
I can look down and spy on her
And overhear her every move.
And every move she makes is slow,
Pushing the popper to and fro.
I hear the corn begin to pop.
O sing, white church, that Christ is born.
I do not hear your singing choir,
I only hear the popping corn
Until I hear the popping stop.
But now, praise be, I more than hear it,
For lifted on the breath of fire
The fragrance rises like pure spirit.
The fragrance rises while the snow
Is falling, falling long ago.

Homeward

Sun that gives the world its color,
Turn me darker, deeper, duller.

Make the clouds white, and the foam.
Make me brown as fresh turned loam.

Save whiteness for sky and sea.
Give the tan of earth to me.

Blend me to the hue of loam.
Turn me homeward, turn me home.

Earthworm

My spading fork turning the earth turns
This fellow out—without touching him this time.
Robbed of all resistance to his progress
He squirms awhile in the too-easy air
Before an ancient and implicit purpose
Starts him traveling in one direction
Reaching out, contracting, reaching out,
Contracting—a clean and glistening earth-pink.
He has turned more earth than I have with my fork.
He has lifted more earth than all men have or will.
Breaking the earth in spring men break his body.
And it is broken in the beaks of birds.
He has become and will again become
The flying and singing of birds. Yet another spring
I shall find him working noiselessly in the earth.
When I am earth again he will be there.

Old Man Feeding Hens

The oldest looking man, the slowest moving,
I ever saw, dressed all in somber black
And with a great December-snowdrift beard,
Leans on a staff and with his other hand
Feeds a few Barred-Rock hens from a slung basket.

Neither the man nor hens make any sound
For me to overhear. One might suppose
That he had passed beyond the need of words,
Either to speak them or to hear them spoken,
And that his hens had grown into his silence.

The house beside him is a Barred-Rock gray
With not one windowsign of habitation.
Some day and soon it will have less than none,
And on that day the hens may not be fed
Till noon or evening or the second morning.

That Dark Other Mountain

My father could go down a mountain faster than I
Though I was first one up.
Legs braced or with quick steps he slid the gravel slopes
Where I picked cautious footholds.

Black, Iron, Eagle, Doublehead, Chocorua,
Wildcat and Carter Dome—
He beat me down them all. And that last other mountain.
And that dark other mountain.

He Mourned, But Not As Others Mourn

He mourned, but not as others mourn.
One death was not a cause for two.
All that was deadly was his scorn
For what grief does and does not do.

Now we must live a little less,
Dilute the joys our dead will miss—
Such grief he counted spinelessness.
Called it not grief but cowardice.

With lives his friends had to defer
He filled his own life to the brim.
For them he lived the livelier,
And they, the lovelier in him.

And all the days and all the years
Loved ones had loved but had not known
He fashioned into bright careers,
He made them blossom as his own.

We mourn, but not as he would mourn,
For he is dead. But does he rest?
No one can bear what he has borne.
No friend can shoulder his bequest.

The Goldfish Bowl

The year is nineteen forty-one, the season winter.
The earth lies naked to the wind. The frost goes deep.
Along the river shore the ice-sheets creak and splinter.
Under the frost the tree roots and the woodchuck sleep.

The time is winter night, but in the swimming pool
Is summer noontime, noon by the electric sun.
The young men dive, emerge, and float a while, and fool,
And dive again. The year is nineteen forty-one.

The tropic water is safe-filtered and the room
Is air-conditioned, kept an even eighty-five.
Outdoors a shivering newsboy is proclaiming doom.
Inside the pool a naked youth is poised to dive.

The time is ten o'clock in nineteen forty-one.
Somewhere a bell upon a tower begins to toll
While hour by hour the moon, its fat face warm with sun,
Gloats like a patient cat above a goldfish bowl.

Distance and Peace

Go far enough away from anything
In time or space (and space is only time)
And you have peace. The clashes of the stars
Do not disturb the starlit night of earth.
And earthly wars if they are old enough
Make restful reading to a man in bed.

And so with distance that is neither space
Nor time. The grass we walk upon is peaceful.
We can lie down on it and go to sleep,
Being too far above it ever to feel
The toil and competition of the roots,
Their struggle, slow frustration and defeat.

Walls

A passerby might just as well be blind.
These walls are walls no passer sees behind.
Or wants or needs to want to see behind.
Let the walls hide what they are there to bind.
Out-of-sight they say is out-of-mind.
The walls are cruel and the walls are kind.

If We Had Known

If we had known all that we know
We never would have let him go.

He never would have reached the river
If we had guessed his going. Never.

We had the stronger argument
Had we but dreamed his dark intent.

Or if our words failed to dissuade him
Unarguing love might still have stayed him.

We would have lured him from his course.
And if love failed, there still was force.

We would have locked the door and barred it.
We would have stood all night to guard it.

But what we know, we did not know.
We said good-bye and saw him go.

While I Slept

While I slept, while I slept and the night grew colder
She would come to my bedroom stepping softly
And draw a blanket about my shoulder
While I slept.

While I slept, while I slept in the dark still heat
She would come to my bedside stepping coolly
And smooth the twisted troubled sheet
While I slept.

Now she sleeps, sleeps under quiet rain
While nights grow warm or nights grow colder
And I wake and sleep and wake again
While she sleeps.

Unanimity

On shipboard and far out at sea
Two sat in deck chairs drawn together
Reading the same book silently
Day after day of even weather.

One held the book for both to read
And turned the page when it was read—
Two minds so equal and agreed
That nothing needed to be said.

The Hound

Life the hound
Equivocal
Comes at a bound
Either to rend me
Or to befriend me.
I cannot tell
The hound's intent
Till he has sprung
At my bare hand
With teeth or tongue.
Meanwhile I stand
And wait the event.

Diver

Diver go down
Down through the green
Inverted dawn
To the dark unseen
To the never day
The under night
Starless and steep
Deep beneath deep
Diver fall
And falling fight
Your weed-dense way
Until you crawl
Until you touch
Weird water land
And stand.

Diver come up
Up through the green
Into the light
The sun   the seen
But in the clutch
Of your dripping hand
Diver bring
Some uncouth thing
That we could swear
And would have sworn
Was never born
Or could ever be
Anywhere
Blaze on our sight
Make us see.

Summons

Keep me from going to sleep too soon
Or if I go to sleep too soon
Come wake me up. Come any hour
Of night. Come whistling up the road.
Stomp on the porch. Bang on the door.
Make me get out of bed and come
And let you in and light a light.
Tell me the northern lights are on
And make me look. Or tell me clouds
Are doing something to the moon
They never did before, and show me.
See that I see. Talk to me till
I'm half as wide awake as you
And start to dress wondering why
I ever went to bed at all.
Tell me the walking is superb.
Not only tell me but persuade me.
You know I'm not too hard persuaded.

Coming and Going

The crows are cawing,
The cocks are crowing,
The roads are thawing,
The boys are thumbing,
The winds are blowing,
The year is coming.

The jays are jawing,
The cows are lowing,
The trees are turning,
The saws are sawing,
The fires are burning,
The year is going.

Biography

Speak the truth
And say I am slow,
Slow to outgrow
A backward youth.

Slow to see,
Slow to believe,
Slow to achieve,
Slow to be.

Yet being slow
Has recompense:
The present tense.
Say that I grow.

Excellence

Excellence is millimeters and not miles.
From poor to good is great. From good to best is small.
From almost best to best sometimes not measurable.
The man who leaps the highest leaps perhaps an inch
Above the runner-up. How glorious that inch
And that split-second longer in the air before the fall.

Nothing Is Far

Though I have never caught the word
Of God from any calling bird,
I hear all that the ancients heard.

Though I have seen no deity
Enter or leave a twilit tree,
I see all that the seers see.

A common stone can still reveal
Something not stone, not seen, yet real.
What may a common stone conceal?

Nothing is far that once was near.
Nothing is hid that once was clear.
Nothing was God that is not here.

Here is the bird, the tree, the stone.
Here in the sun I sit alone
Between the known and the unknown.

Index of First Lines

How deep is his duplicity who in a flash, *53*
How flawless and unvarying his candor, *43*
I am not flattered that a bell, *94*
I follow Plato only with my mind, *116*
If to the taunting peneplain the peak, *54*
If you have watched a moulting mantis, *23*
If we had known all that we know, *129*
Indian-wise, *46*
In mythology the restraint shown by dolphins, *8*
Interrupted fern we call it, *94*
In this soft age, in my soft, *76*
Ireland which the sea refuses, *10*
It contains nothing, *37*
It is a little thing to die, *119*
Just before night darkens to total night, *72*
Keep me from going to sleep too soon, *134*
Life the hound, *132*
Lingo of birds was easier than the lingo of peasants, *24*
Moving unmoved, *84*
My father could go down a mountain faster than I, *124*
My spading fork turning the earth turns, *122*
Nature and God by some elusive yet felicitous, *69*
Night comes no wilier inch-wise step-wise, *70*
November seemed to haunt the place, *103*
Observe how he negotiates his way, *56*
Old men weigh too much or weigh, *4*
Once I observed a serpent climb a tree, *92*
Only a fierce, *14*
Only in the perfection of his calligraphy, *45*
On shipboard and far out at sea, *131*
Others have moved the heavens, *19*
O world of Toms—tomfools, Tom Peppers, *59*
Pioneer, paratrooper, missionary of the gospel seed, *87*
Presto, pronto! Two boys, two horses, *62*
Sailboat, your secret. With what dove-and-serpent, *51*
Searock his tower above the sea, *41*
Sing a song of juniper, *106*
So bandit-eyed, so undovelike a bird, *71*
Speak the truth, *136*
Suddenly all the gold I ever wanted, *67*
Sun that gives the world its color, *121*